Richmond upon Thames Libraries

Renew online at www.richmond.gov.uk/libraries

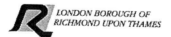

LONDON BOROUGH OF
RICHMOND UPON THAMES

Barney
the Horse
and other tales from the farm

Books by Michael Morpurgo

michael morpurgo

Barney
the Horse
and other tales from the farm

Illustrated by Guy Parker-Rees

HarperCollins *Children's Books*

First published in the United Kingdom by
HarperCollins *Children's Books* in 2022
HarperCollins *Children's Books* is a division of HarperCollins*Publishers* Ltd
1 London Bridge Street
London SE1 9GF

www.harpercollins.co.uk

HarperCollins*Publishers*
1st Floor, Watermarque Building, Ringsend Road
Dublin 4, Ireland

1

ISBN 978–0–00–845151–6

For Joan, who made Nethercott so special

Contents

MISSING!

I'm not very good at talking. My mouth goes

all stiff if I try, and I stutter. Everyone kept

asking me questions – the policewoman, the

farmer, my friends. My teacher, Mr Morrison,

never made me talk if I didn't want to. He

crouched down beside me and said I didn't

have to tell people about it if I didn't want

to, but maybe I could write it all down,

everything that had happened. I like writing –
I don't stutter when I write. So I did. Here it
is, Mr Morrison. No stuttering.

'I had a real adventure today. It began before
breakfast. We are down at the farm, you
and me and the rest of my class, staying at
Nethercott House like we always do every
year, doing farming stuff like feeding hens
and ducks and geese, and calves and sheep
and pigs. We do a lot of feeding, and I like
doing it. We all do, except it smells a bit –
sometimes a lot.

Anyway, it was our turn to get up early

and go with you and the farmer to feed the

sheep and count the lambs. We have to feed

the mother sheep – ewes, they're called – so

they can make milk to feed their lambs. So we

all had sacks of corn and we emptied the corn

into the trough, which isn't easy because the

ewes push and shove a lot. But I liked that bit,

because you can stand there and push your

fingers deep down into their greasy wool,

and then stroke them, and they don't mind

because they're too busy eating to worry

about you.

And then we had to stand back and count the sheep and the lambs, just in case any had gone missing or were ill or something. There should have been twenty-six ewes, and sixty-one lambs. We counted twenty-six ewes – that was easy and we all agreed on the number. But none of us could count more than sixty lambs. We checked and we checked. One was definitely missing.

So the farmer sent us off to look for it. It was a ram lamb, the farmer said – a boy lamb. There were foxes and crows about that could attack him, and without his mother to feed him he'd soon be in trouble. So we had to find him, and quick.

"The first to find him will be 'farmer of the day'," you said. And I really wanted to be farmer of the day. We get a badge for that, and I like badges.

So off we went in ones and twos all around the field. I went in ones, on my own.

23

The lamb wasn't lying down sick in the

grass by the hedge.

He wasn't caught

up in the wire.

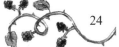

The farmer told us to look in the corner

of the field especially.

They like the shelter there, he said, from

the sun or the wind or the rain.

I looked, but the lamb wasn't there. I looked all around. Everyone else was out of sight by now.

There was a wood below the field,

Bluebell Wood we call it. I never saw so

many bluebells in all my life – thousands,

millions, probably – and I love the smell of

28

them as you walk through. So I went looking

there, because I thought the lamb might

like the smell too. I thought he could have

clambered over the hedge into the wood.

29

I saw some wool caught up on a twig there,

and I found a hole he could have gone

through.

I crawled through, and there I was in

Bluebell Wood.

 I called for him,

looked for him,

 listened for him.

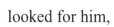

31

All I saw was a carpet of bluebells, and all I heard was the wind in the trees. I thought of turning back, of joining the others. But I really wanted to be farmer of the day, so I kept looking.

I walked down past the badgers' dens,
through the bluebells to the stream at the
bottom. I didn't see a badger, but I saw a deer
springing away – they have white bottoms.

I saw a heron take off as I reached the

water. Prehistoric, they are, like pterodactyls.

And then I saw him. The lamb was lying

there under a tree, but he was on the other

side of the stream.

I didn't run. The farmer had told us never

to frighten the sheep. So I walked slowly

down the hill, talking to him softly as I came,

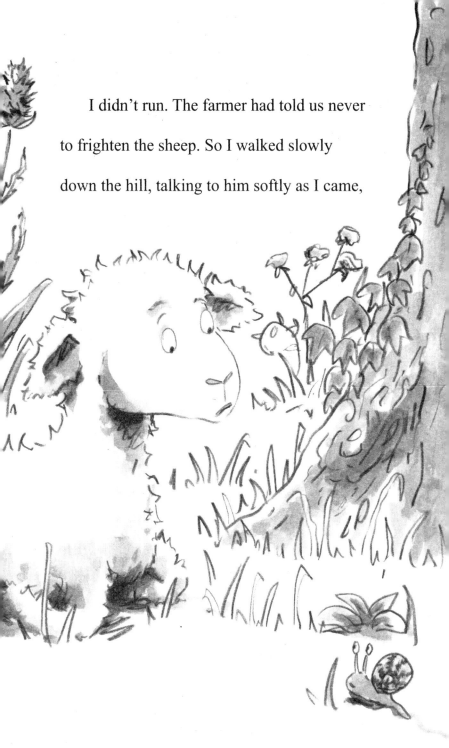

so as not to alarm him. The stream was wide

and I didn't know how deep. There was no

bridge, not that I could see. The lamb was

soaking wet and shivering. I had to get to him.

He was bleating at me now, calling for help.

So, I tried to find a shallow place to cross

and waded out into the stream. The water

came over my wellies. I kept wading.

It came up to my waist. I kept going.

Then I slipped and lost my footing, and

suddenly I was being carried along. I could

swim, I thought, so I'd be all right. The lamb

was running along the bank, still bleating at

me. My wellies would not let me swim. I was

being dragged down.

And then there was a branch. It was like
it was reaching out to me. I grabbed it, held

on and hauled myself

out on to the bank.

Then I was lying

there, coughing and

spluttering, but alive.

And the lamb was right

beside me. He was safe. I was safe. All I

had to do was get him

back to Nethercott

now, and I'd be

farmer of

the day.

So I started walking, and he just followed me, like a dog, but bleating instead of barking. The trouble was that we were still on the wrong side of the stream, and I did not want to risk trying to swim back across again. And, anyway, how could I with the lamb? I couldn't swim and carry him.

We walked on and on through the wood
and out into the field on the other side – a
field full of cows that came plodding towards
us. Then they were trotting. Then they were

running, galloping. It was a stampede! We

ran for it then, the lamb and me, and they ran

after us. There was a hut down by the river. It

was our only hope.

The door wasn't locked, thank goodness.
So we hid inside that hut. Out of the window I
could see the cows all around outside, tossing
their heads and mooing. And there with them
was the bull, with the ring in his nose.

George, the farmer called

him. He was pawing the ground. There was

no way I was going to leave that hut until

George was gone – until they were all gone.

47

So, we stayed there, the lamb and me. I talked to him and he bleated to me. We had a talk about this and that. I told him all about home in Bermondsey in London, that there were no sheep there. I told him about my mum not being well, but that the doctor said she'd be better soon. I never stuttered once talking to that lamb, not once. Funny that.

I don't know what he bleated to me. I think it was that he was cold and hungry. I took him on my lap to keep him warm, and told him we'd find his mum again soon and that she'd feed him. He seemed to understand. Soft, he was. Lovely.

I was wet through and cold, but I thought I'd stay put until someone came looking for us, that it would be safer that way.

Someone did come, a long while later, but it wasn't you or the farmer, and it wasn't the other children. It was a helicopter. I heard it coming over. I looked out of the window.

The cows and the bull were nowhere to be seen. I picked up the lamb, opened the door of the shed and ran out, waving and shouting at the helicopter.

You know the rest of the story – how they picked me and the lamb up and flew us

back to Nethercott House, how we landed in the field and all the children and the teachers were there, including you, Mr Morrison, all cheering and waving, and I felt a little bit like a hero. I liked that feeling. A lot.

The farmer was there too to take the lamb

off me. "You gave us all quite a fright," he

said. "But thanks. Proper farmer, you are."

So, that evening I was made farmer of the

day, and I got my badge. And my lamb was

with his mum, and everything was all right.'

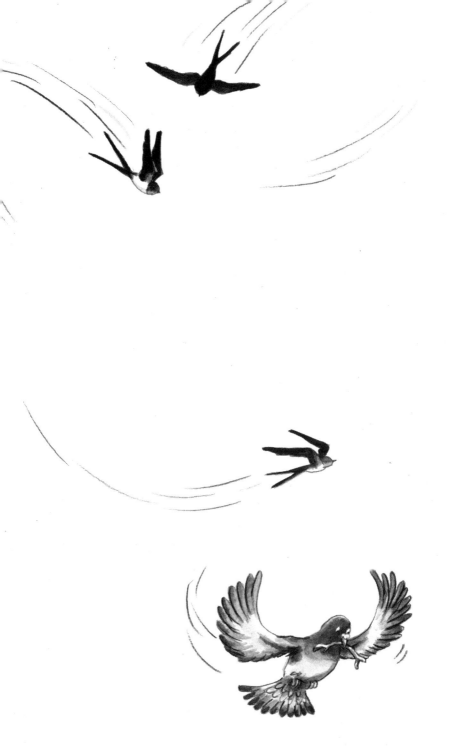

BIRD BOY

Matt loved Nethercott House, the huge

rambling house they were staying in. He

loved its towering chimneys, its long echoing

corridors, wide staircases and secret rooms,

the views of the hills from the window of

his dormitory – not a house in sight – and he

loved stories in the evening in front of the

log fire.

But he didn't like being away from home.

He missed his room, his dad and his mum. He

didn't miss TV, but he did miss his football.

He missed Molly too, his little sister, who

would jump on him first thing in the morning

to wake him up and was more than sometimes

a bit of a pest. But she was three.

It was Matt's first time away from home,

first time in the countryside, first time on a

farm, first time on a

bunk bed, first time

tramping down

muddy lanes,

first time taking

eggs out from

under a hen, first time

picking gooseberries or

blackcurrants. It was

the first time he'd

eaten the beans he'd

picked himself from

the vegetable garden, the first time he'd spent a whole week in wellies, the first time he'd fed a calf or a pig, the first time he'd groomed a horse or helped bring a newborn lamb into the world. He loved all that, loved being a farmer.

But what he liked best of all was just

being out in the countryside. He loved

climbing to the top of the hill and standing

there in the wind, puffed out. And he loved

the birds.

He'd always
loved birds. At home,
outside his high-rise
flat on the seventeenth
floor, there was a
beautiful grey pigeon
who came to visit.
She'd perch outside
his bedroom window,
which looked out
over the walkway,
and sometimes shelter
there for a long time.
Once, he'd seen a

whole pigeon love

story going on out

there. Her boyfriends

came visiting, bringing

twigs to make her

a nest on the ledge

above the window,

and one by one they

paraded up and down,

showing off their

twigs, puffing out their

chest feathers. She

took her pick.

But then it all

went wrong. She chose her mate, and they

built an untidy twiggy nest, and she sat up

there on her eggs, waiting. Two eggs, white.
Matt had a crafty peek from the top of the
stepladder. Matt was longing for the chicks to
hatch. But then, one day, while they were all
out, their horrible neighbour, Mrs Bush, came
out with her broom and just knocked down
the nest, because 'pigeons are dirty things',
she said. There was a big, shouting row in the
walkway, but that didn't help. Matt's pigeon
was gone, the twiggy nest and the eggs too,
and that was that.

There were pigeons out on the farm too,
flying free, nesting where they liked and
cooing when it was warm and sunny, which

it was most days. Everywhere Matt went

there were birds: herons and kingfishers and

cormorants and dippers down by the river;

swifts and swallows and martins over the

fields; crows and rooks in the high elm

trees; blackbirds and wrens and blue tits and

goldfinches in the garden. The whole place

was alive with birds and birdsong. It was

a paradise for Matt. He had listed all the

different birds he had seen and drawn each

one of them. He had his book of birds with him and was looking up every bird he saw. Mr Prentice, their class teacher, called him 'Bird Boy'. And Matt liked that.

But Matt did have a favourite. And it

wasn't a pigeon. It was a swallow.

Matt had found out all about swallows.

He knew that they flew 6,000 miles from

South Africa to England, over tropical

78

rainforests, over African plains where

lions and giraffes and wildebeest roamed,

over deserts where oryx and camels and

snakes and scorpions lived, over the seas

where whales and dolphins whooped, over

mountains where eagles and vultures soared,

all the way dodging the hawks that came

hunting them, until they came, at last, back to

the very same place they were born, the same

barn on the same farm.

And now, in the barn in the stable yard at Nethercott, there was a swallow's nest – hidden away high up, made of dried mud. Mr Prentice had told the children not to go too near, not to disturb the nest, because the chicks had hatched out.

Matt knew that was right and had not gone too close, but close enough sometimes to see five heads peeking out of the nest, beaks wide open and screeching when the parent birds flew in to feed them, again and again and again.

Every spare moment he had, Matt was there at a window or out in the yard watching all the comings and goings. So he was there on the day the chicks left the nest for the first time.

No one had to teach them how to fly –

they just did it, easily,

acrobatically, balletically,

slicing through the air.

They chased each other round and round the yard. Matt could see they were loving every moment of it. Counting them was difficult, because they were endlessly criss-crossing

each other in the air, twisting and turning at

such speed that he could never be sure how

many there were. Was it four or five young

ones? And were the parent birds flying with

them? It should be seven in all.

Then there came a moment when they

all settled side by side on the hip of the roof

above the stable. Four, only four young ones,

and the mother and father flying proudly over

their heads. One was missing. Matt went to

check the nest. One was still there, teetering

on the edge, wings trying themselves out.

Matt could see he was thinking about it,

daring himself to take off and join the others,

but he wasn't sure his wings would hold him

up. Matt knew he mustn't get too close or it

would make things worse. He backed away to

the far side of the yard, crouched down under

the kitchen window and watched at a distance.

This was when Matt noticed he wasn't the only one watching. The farm cat was there, sitting beside a wheelbarrow right under the nest, eyes fixed upwards, tail swishing, twitching. He was waiting, and Matt knew what he was waiting for.

The swallow that was still on the nest had seen the cat now, and so had the four others. They were racing round and round the yard, the two parent birds frantic, swooping down as close to the cat as they dared, screeching to frighten him away. But the cat sat where he was, taking no notice of them. He was waiting, waiting until the swallow up there panicked and tried to fly before he could. Matt thought of running back across the yard and chasing the cat away, but then he'd frighten the young swallow and he could fall – and if he still couldn't fly, then the cat could get there before him.

It all happened so fast.
Suddenly the swallow
was falling from the nest,
tumbling – then taking
wing and flying, but only
just, over the cat's head,
and coming straight as an
arrow at the window above
Matt's head. The clunk
when the little swallow hit
the glass was sickening. He
fell at Matt's feet, and lay
there. Still.

The cat was running

across the yard towards Matt, towards the

dead swallow.

Matt was not going to let it happen. He

was on his feet and yelling at him. The cat

ran off, but only as far as the wheelbarrow

under the nest, where he sat, waiting again.

He had not given up. The family of swallows

was wheeling and screeching above the yard,

swooping, diving. They had not given up

either.

Matt didn't like to pick up dead things.

But he had to pick up this swallow. He

could not let the cat have him.

He sat down on the cobbles

beside the swallow and

picked him up, cradling

him in his hands.

And that's where the

other children and Mr Prentice found him

a while later, sitting there under the kitchen

window. Matt didn't like to look up because

he'd been crying.

All the children were crowding round

now to get a closer look. No one said a

word. Then at last Matt looked up, and they

could all see his tears. But, what

was strange is that he was

smiling. 'He came alive,'

he told them. 'He

was dead, and then

he came alive. I can

feel his heart beating.

Honest.' He opened his cupped hand just enough. 'And look, he can lift his head. And I can feel his claws gripping me, and his wings – they want to fly. But he's not ready. He's too weak. I think he's stunned. He needs to be warm and quiet. I'm going to stay here, holding him, till he flies.'

Mr Prentice told the children that Matt was right, that the bird needed quiet. So he took them to the other side of the yard where they all sat down and watched in silence. But, before he sat down himself, he went and chased the cat away.

In time – and it took a long time –

Matt could feel the swallow stirring in his hands, the claws gripping tighter, the wings struggling more strongly to open, to fly.

And he was holding his head up now, looking around him with his bright little eyes.

Above him, his family were perched on the roof and waiting, sometimes flying down over the yard, over the children and over Matt, who was holding in his hands, they knew, the last member of their family.

The chick kept looking up at them, opening his beak, calling to them, and all the time he was growing stronger in the warmth of Matt's hands.

'He's ready, I think,' Matt said, getting

slowly, carefully to his feet. He had one last

look down at the swallow, and the swallow

had one last look up at him. Then Matt lifted

his arms, opened his hands and away the

swallow went, up to join the rest of his family.

They whirled and wheeled round the yard,

flew up over the roof and were gone.

There was clapping from inside the kitchen,

where everyone had been watching, and

whooping and cheering from all the children.

Mr Prentice was so moved he couldn't say

anything, so he ruffled Matt's hair instead.

The swallows were still using the nest as

their home all the rest of the week they were

at Nethercott. So Matt was out there watching

them hour after hour.

On the last morning they were all on the coach, ready to leave for home, but Matt was missing. Mr Prentice knew where he'd be, and went to fetch him. He was in the yard, of course, watching the swallows, all seven of them, swooping and soaring above.

'Do you know which is yours, Bird Boy?'
Mr Prentice asked.

'No,' Matt told him, 'not really, sir. But it
doesn't matter. He's alive, that's what matters.
And they'll all be back next year, back from
Africa. This is their home. And I'll be back
too. I'm coming again next year.'

'Me too,' said Mr Prentice.

GO FOR IT!

My grandma was the start of it. She was

the start of me, too, if you see what I'm

saying. I mean grandmas are the start of all

of us, in a way. We wouldn't be here without

them, after all. And I wouldn't be who I am,

nor what I am, nor where I am, without my grandma. That's for sure.

Don't get me wrong. Mum was good to me, the best mum I could have had. But she had to go out to work. So Grandma lived with us and looked after me a lot. My dad wasn't there. Dad had been in the army, and he'd been killed before I was born. Mum had a favourite photo of Dad in his army uniform on his horse. She kept that photo and his beret on a table in her bedroom. She was sad sometimes about Dad. I missed Dad, but it wasn't so bad for me, because I never knew him. I've seen him on video, riding his horse.

There's a team of six horses pulling the

gun. And he's riding the front horse.

And I've seen another video of him holding me in his arms when I was a baby. So I know how he looked, how he sounded, how he laughed. But he wasn't there when I was growing up. Grandma was, all the time. And she was my dad's mum.

You have to know a bit more about my grandma. When she was very little her dad was a milkman, and he'd go around the streets of Stoke with his horse and cart delivering the milk. He was the last

milkman in Stoke like that, still delivering

his milk by horse and cart. And sometimes,

in the school holidays, Grandma would go

with him. She'd help carry the

bottles to the doorsteps and

bring back the empties, or

she'd lead the horse from

house to house. Best of

all, whenever her dad

would lift her up, she'd ride

the horse home. He was called

Barney. He was black and white and big.

She'd spend every hour she could with that

horse, cleaning out his stable, grooming him,

talking to him. Grandma said she told more

secrets to Barney than to anyone else.

By the time she left school, Grandma knew exactly what she wanted to do. She wanted to work with horses. She got a job living and working on a farm where they also kept horses – racing horses. She looked after them and rode them out on the gallops, helped with all their training and exercising. She was the only girl working in the stables. The others, all the stable boys and the jockeys, teased her quite a bit. She didn't like it, but she never let it bother her too much. She could ride as well as they could. She knew it, and they knew it.

What really upset her was what happened

when it came to taking the horses to the races.

She'd groom them and always turn them out

smart and shining, looking their best every

time, and she'd lead them round the paddock.

But she was never once allowed to ride

them in a race, never allowed to be a proper

jockey, and that was because she was a girl. It

was a rule in those days. No girl jockeys.

After a while she decided she'd had enough of this and she complained to the trainer, who was her boss. She said it was unfair and wrong, that girls mattered as much as boys, and could ride just as well as boys. There was a big argument, and she was sacked.

Grandma told me that story often.

'Always remember,' she'd say to me, 'you stand up for what's right. And always remember that people matter. Every one of us matters. And you know what my motto is? "Go for it!"'

131

It was Grandma who said I should go to the farm on the school trip. This was in my last year at Turves Green Junior School. I said I didn't want to, that I liked being at home. And that was true – I knew I'd be homesick. But Grandma said I should 'go for it', and that she would pay for it. It would be my birthday present.

So that's how, in the end, I went on the trip to Wick with all my school friends. I was sick on the bus, but once we got there I wasn't at all homesick. We were staying in this huge old house, fifteen rooms I counted, where the bats flew around in the evening, and we had stories in front of the log fire.

We slept in dormitories and got woken up

by the birds in the morning, we picked apples

and blackberries,

we went milking the cows, and . . . and . . .

we looked after the horses.

I'd never been near a horse before, except in Grandma's horse stories – about riding Barney the milk horse, about wanting to be a jockey. It was because of Grandma's stories, and because she made me go to Wick that I fell in love with one of the horses there. And that horse changed my life.

This is the weirdest thing. The horse I looked after at Wick was called Barney, and he was black and white and big, just like Grandma's horse when she was little.

Once I'd met Barney, I hardly noticed anything else – not the ducks, geese and hens, not the cows and sheep. I spent every minute

I could watching him out there grazing in the

orchard.

I'd be brushing him,

combing his mane,

picking out his feet.

They let me look after his saddle and his reins and his stirrups. I talked to him, told him about Mum being sad about Dad, told him Grandma's story. He listened, he really listened.

I loved it when he yawned because I could

see all his teeth, which needed a good

cleaning. I loved it when he chomped his hay,

when he slurped his water, and especially

when he farted!

He did that quite a lot, especially when I led

him out into the orchard and let him go. He

loved a good roll in the grass, and then he'd

race round chasing the other horses, kicking

up his back legs – and, yes, farting.

For that week at the farm, at Wick, Barney was my horse. But my love for him has lasted all my life, in a way. I'm now thirty-three years old, and I've got a family of my own.

I've got a three-year-old son, and, yes, he's called Barney too! But, before I did all that, I did what Grandma advised me to: I went for it!

Once I left school, I did exactly what she had done. I went to work in a riding stable just on the edge of town, mucking out, cleaning all the tack, looking after the saddles and bridles and reins. I got paid, of course, but I also got to ride every day for as long as I could. And soon enough I was teaching other people to ride, kids usually. I started competing at shows. I started winning.

I loved every minute of it. I lived with the horses too, sort of, in a room above the stables.

I was lying there one night in my bed and thinking of that photo at home, of Dad in his uniform on his horse, and I was wondering. It was the horses I loved, not the competing or the winning. I just wanted to be with the horses, be like my dad was.

The more I thought about my new idea, the more I wanted to do it. I found out they needed women in the army as much as men. It seemed the right thing to do. I'd be working with horses, and I'd be a soldier just like Dad

had been, I'd be wearing the same uniform.

I knew I'd feel closer to him somehow, and I

wanted that very much. I think I'd wanted that

ever since I was little, when he wasn't there.

I knew Grandma wouldn't mind. But I

was worried what Mum would think. I didn't

want to make her upset or sad. She'd had

enough of that. She cried when I told her, but she wasn't sad, not at all. 'Your dad would have been so proud,' she said. 'Like I am.'

So, I joined the army, as a trooper, in the Royal Horse Artillery, helping to pull the guns whenever we were needed. I was a proper soldier too, we all were. But my time with the horses was always the best time for me.

Grandma and Mum came down to London to see me once in the park, firing our guns for the Queen's birthday. I always felt Dad was there too – hoped he was.

I've thought about Grandma a lot over the years, about how unfair and wrong it was that she never had the opportunities I've had, about how she helped me go to the farm at Wick, and how that changed my life. Before mounting up to go off on duty, I often wish that Grandma could see me now. And I remember the two Barneys, Grandma's in Stoke when she was little, and mine at Wick when I was little. I always make it a routine of mine to say to myself, before we set off with the guns, to steel my nerves, to gee myself up, 'Go for it, girl. Go for it!'

Thanks, Grandma. Thanks, Mum, and Dad.

And thanks, Wick, and thanks to all you

Barneys – all three, my little Barney too.

(Three years old and he's riding already!)

Oh, lucky me!

Farms for City Children

The stories in this book are inspired by school visits to Farms for City Children.

Farms for City Children was founded in 1976 by Clare and Michael Morpurgo. The charity offers urban children the opportunity

to live and work on a real farm! Since then more than one hundred thousand children have visited one of the farms – Wick Court in Gloucestershire, Lower Treginnis in Pembrokeshire or Nethercott House in Devon. Spending time as farmers brings great joy, new discoveries and the opportunity to reconnect with nature, friends and teachers. For many, it is the most memorable time of their young lives.

You can find out more about coming to stay on the farms here:

www.farmsforcitychildren.org

WICK COURT IN GLOUCESTERSHIRE

ALL SORTS of animals live in the farmyard
behind the tumble-down barn
on Mudpuddle Farm . . .

Join the fun on the farm, with:

Mossop the old farm cat

Albertine the goose

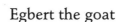

Jigger the sheepdog

Pintsize the piglet

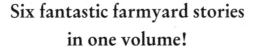

Egbert the goat

and Farmer Rafferty!

Six fantastic farmyard stories
in one volume!

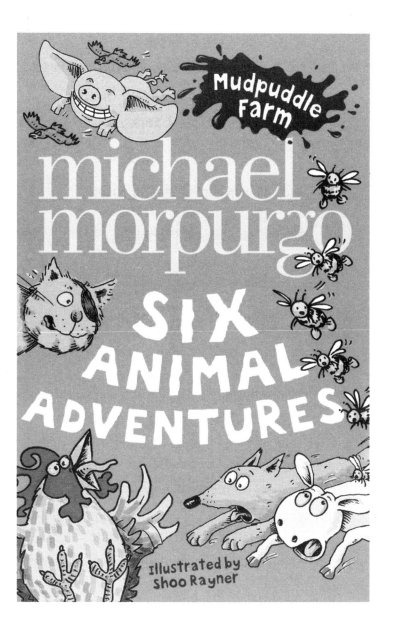

Mudpuddle
Farm

michael
morpurgo

SIX
ANIMAL
ADVENTURES

Illustrated by
Shoo Rayner